Ladybird

This Little Story
belongs to

Sally Dellin

56

Published by Ladybird Books Ltd
27 Wrights Lane London W8 5TZ
A Penguin Company
3 5 7 9 10 8 6 4

© LADYBIRD BOOKS LTD MCMXCVIII

Printed in Italy

Cheeky
Little
Kitten

by Joan Stimson
illustrated by Jan Smith

Little Kitten was the cheekiest, cheeriest cat in the entire neighbourhood. He thought up the most brilliant games. He never ran out of jokes and, whenever Little Kitten was around, it was almost impossible… not to smile.

But one day a new tabby cat came to the neighbourhood. She was snooty and sniffy. She was vain and a pain. And right from the start the new cat made it clear. She was too busy worrying about her looks to enjoy herself.

"Don't take any notice," said all Little Kitten's friends.

Have you heard the one about...

But Little Kitten couldn't bear to
think of anyone not having fun. So
next day he bounded up to the new
cat with a cheerful,

*"Tabby Scowler, come and play.
Try a smile and make my day!"*

And then he began to tell his
cheekiest puppy joke.

Little Kitten's friends laughed so loudly that he could hardly hear himself speak. Tabby Scowler thought the joke was funny too. But then she remembered.

"I've just arranged my whiskers. And, if I have a good laugh, they'll get in a tangle again."

So, instead of joining in, Tabby
Scowler simply scowled some more.
And stuck her nose in the air.

I mustn't get
my whiskers in
a twist.

Little Kitten was disappointed. But next day he bounded up to the new cat with a cheerful,

*"Tabby Scowler, come and play.
Try a smile and make my day!"*

And then he began to describe his latest game.

"It's called *Run, Wriggle and Roll*," said Little Kitten.

His friends were already purring expectantly. But Tabby Scowler looked confused. So Little Kitten explained.

"Run round the garden, wriggle through the hedge and roll down the bank."

Whoooosh! The other cats all rushed off together.

Don't get left behind, Tabby Scowler!

For a moment Tabby Scowler was caught up in the excitement too. But, as the other cats disappeared into the hedge, she remembered.

"I've just washed my fur. And, if I wriggle and roll, it will get all messy again."

So, instead of joining in, Tabby Scowler simply scowled some more. And stuck her nose in the air.

Little Kitten was shocked. But that evening he bounded up to the new cat with a cheerful,

*"Tabby Scowler, come and play.
Try a smile and make my day!"*

And then he began to set up his moonlight shadow show.

Tabby Scowler thought perhaps she could make an exciting shadow shape too. But then she remembered.

"I've just draped myself elegantly over the wall. And, if I twist my tail into a snake, I might not be able to make it elegant again."

So, instead of joining in, Tabby Scowler simply scowled some more. And stuck her nose in the air.

Little Kitten was beside himself.

"Don't give her a second thought," said all his friends.

But Little Kitten was determined.

"I'll make that cat enjoy herself," he announced, "if it's the last thing I do."

Next day Little Kitten waited patiently for his chance. And that afternoon he *crept* up to the new cat... in total silence.

The sun was warm. And Tabby Scowler was taking a cat nap.

"If I can just find her tickle spot," thought Cheeky Little Kitten to himself, "then she's bound to burst out..."

"How *DARE* you disturb my beauty sleep!" roared Tabby Scowler. And suddenly she was wide-awake and furious!

Tabby Scowler chased Little Kitten right round the garden. She leapt after him as he dived for the safety of the hedge. And, when he rolled head over paws down the bank, Tabby Scowler somersaulted after him.

By the time she caught up with Little Kitten, Tabby Scowler was a changed cat.

"He's gone too far this time," groaned all Little Kitten's friends.

"Shall I help you re-arrange your whiskers?" asked Little Kitten.

"*NO!*" bellowed Tabby Scowler. "I'm enjoying myself far too much to worry about my whiskers," she explained. "And after that *AMAZING* chase, I'm in the mood for a good joke."

I haven't ad so much fun for ages!

"Now," she nudged Little Kitten, "have you heard the one about the puppy from Peru?"

Little Kitten shook his head in astonishment.

"Well," went on the new cat,

> *"There once was a puppy I knew,*
> *Who lived on the plains of Peru.*
> *He wasn't too bright,*
> *But he danced every night*
> *As he dined upon dinosaur stew!"*

Then she rolled around the grass in hysterics.

It made Cheeky Little Kitten's day to see the new cat enjoying herself.

And, from then on, whenever he thought up a new game, Little Kitten could be sure… that Tabby *Smiler* would be the first to join in!